To Jemma

A catalogue record for this book is available from the British Library

Published by Ladybird Books Ltd Loughborough Leicestershire UK
Ladybird Books Ltd is a subsidiary of the Penguin Group of companies
Copyright text © Karen King MCMXCVI
© LADYBIRD BOOKS LTD MCMXCVI
LADYBIRD and the device of a Ladybird are trademarks of Ladybird Books Ltd

Kelly
and the
mermaid

by Karen King ◆ *illustrated by* Jan Lewis

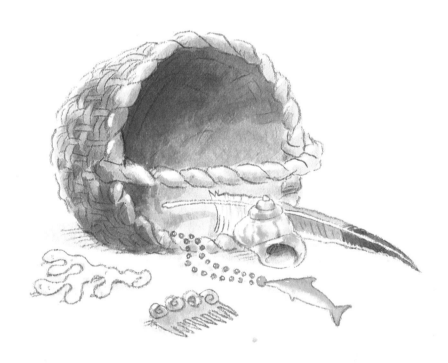

Picture
Ladybird

It was Kelly's birthday. She had been given some lovely presents, but best of all were a blue dolphin necklace and a pretty pink basket.

Kelly put on the necklace, picked up her basket and asked if she could go down to the nearby beach to collect shells.

"Yes, but don't go near the water," said her mum, "and don't be late for your birthday party!"

While she was looking for shells, Kelly lost her necklace. She looked everywhere, but couldn't find it, and was so sad she started to cry.

"Don't cry, little girl," said
someone from behind the rock.

It was a mermaid!
Kelly told the mermaid how she
had just lost her birthday necklace.

"Oh, that's a shame," said the
mermaid. "But don't be sad.
Here's another present instead."
She took one of the shell combs
out of her hair and gave it to Kelly.

Here,
have this!

"Thank you," said Kelly, putting the pretty comb in her basket. "But I'd really like to find my necklace."

"Then I'll help you," said the mermaid.

So they set off. The mermaid searched the rock pools left behind when the tide went out, and Kelly looked all over the sand.

"I'm afraid not," said the crab.
He dug down into the water and
returned with a piece of coral.

"Here, have this instead,"
he said, giving it to Kelly.
"Happy birthday!"

"Thank you," said Kelly, putting the lovely coral in her basket with the comb, "but I'd really like to find my necklace."

The crab offered to help, too, so they set off.

The crab looked under the rocks that were scattered over the beach, while the mermaid explored the rock pools and Kelly searched the sand.

They searched and searched,
The necklace must be near.
Then the mermaid called out…

No!
It was a starfish.

When the starfish heard about
Kelly's lost necklace he gave her
a pretty pearl shell that shone
with rainbow colours.

"Here you are. Have this for your
birthday instead," he said.

"Thank you," said Kelly, putting it in her basket, with the coral and the comb. "But I'd really like to find my necklace."

So the starfish looked under the clumps of seaweed that were scattered on the beach, while the crab rummaged under the rocks, the mermaid swam through the rock pools and Kelly searched the sand.

They searched and searched,
The necklace must be near.
Then the mermaid called out…

Is it here?

No!
It was a seagull.
The mermaid explained that Kelly had
lost her birthday necklace.

"Never mind," said the seagull, plucking a feather from his tail. "Have this instead. Happy birthday!"

"Thank you," said Kelly, putting it in her basket, with the shell, the coral and the mermaid's comb. "But I'd really like to find my necklace."

"Let's all have one last look,"
said the mermaid.

So the seagull flew over the
beach, while the crab turned over
the rocks, the starfish poked
under the clumps of seaweed,
the mermaid searched the rock
pools and Kelly looked in the sand.

They searched and searched,
The necklace must be near.
Then the mermaid called out…

Yes! Here it is!
Kelly was *so* pleased…

The mermaid and the crab and
the starfish and the seagull all
cheered as Kelly picked up
the necklace and put it round
her neck once more.

"Thank you all for your help and the wonderful presents you've given me," she said. "You've been very kind."

The seagull flew up to the cliffs. The crab crawled into a rock pool. The starfish crept under a clump of seaweed, while the mermaid smiled, waved goodbye and disappeared into the sea.

And Kelly ran across the beach, hugging her basket of precious gifts all the way home to her birthday party. It had been her best birthday ever.

Picture Ladybird

Books for reading aloud with 2 – 6 year olds

The exciting *Picture Ladybird* series includes a wide range
of animal stories, funny rhymes, and real life adventures that are
perfect to read aloud and share at storytime or bedtime.

A whole library of beautiful books for you to collect

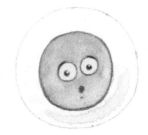

RHYMING STORIES

Easy to follow and great for joining in!

Jasper's Jungle Journey, Val Biro
Shoo Fly, Shoo! Brian Moses
Ten Tall Giraffes, Brian Moses
In Comes the Tide, Valerie King
Toot! Learns to Fly,
Geraldine Taylor & Jill Harker
Who Am I? Judith Nicholls
Fly Eagle, Fly! Jan Pollard

IMAGINATIVE TALES

Mysterious and magical, or just a little shivery

The Star that Fell, Karen Hayles
Wishing Moon, Lesley Harker
Don't Worry William, Christine Morton
This Way Little Badger, Phil McMylor
The Giant Walks, Judith Nicholls
Kelly and the Mermaid, Karen King

FUNNY STORIES

Make storytime good fun!

Benedict Goes to the Beach, Chris Demarest
Bella and Gertie, Geraldine Taylor
Edward Goes Exploring, David Pace
Telephone Ted, Joan Stimson
Top Shelf Ted, Joan Stimson
Helpful Henry, Shen Roddie
What's Wrong with Bertie? Tony Bradman
Bears Can't Fly, Val Biro
Finnigan's Flap, Joan Stimson

REAL LIFE ADVENTURE

Situations to explore and discover

Joe and the Farm Goose,
Geraldine Taylor & Jill Harker
Going to Playgroup,
Geraldine Taylor & Jill Harker
The Great Rabbit Race, Geraldine Taylor
Pushchair Polly, Tony Bradman